The Adventures of Charlie Pierce

The American Jungle

by Harvey E. Oyer III

Illustrations by James Balkovek

Map Illustration by Jeanne Brady

www.TheAdventuresofCharliePierce.com

Become a friend of Charlie Pierce on **Facebook**

Facebook.com/CharliePierceBooks

MIDDLE
RIVER
PRESS

ISBN 0-9817036-0-7

Published by:
Middle River Press
middleriverpress.com
info@middleriverpress.com
Printed in the U.S.A.

Sixth Printing

Dedication

*This book is dedicated to my father, Harvey E. Oyer, Jr., for instilling in me
a love of Florida history and a deep appreciation of our family's role in it.*

Acknowledgments

*I wish to acknowledge the dedicated, outstanding work of my editor, Jon VanZile; my illustrator, James Balkovek;
and my map illustrator, Jeanne Brady; as well as the wonderful people at Middle River Press.
I also wish to thank Dr. Donald W. Curl for granting me permission to use excerpts from
Pioneer Life in Southeast Florida.*

Introduction

This book tells the story of South Florida's early pioneer history through some of the real-life experiences of Charlie Pierce. Pierce's adventures as a young boy were recorded in diaries that he maintained throughout his life. The diaries were later consolidated into a manuscript. To write this book, the author, who is the great-grandnephew of Charlie Pierce, utilized that manuscript, as well as stories passed down through five generations of his family.

From the time of his arrival in 1872 at the age of eight until his death in 1939, Charlie Pierce led one of the most intriguing and exotic lives imaginable. His adventures as a young boy growing up in the wild, untamed frontier of Florida became legendary. Perhaps no other man in Florida's history experienced firsthand as many important events and met as many influential characters as he did.

Charles W. "Charlie" Pierce was born in 1864 in Waukegan, Illinois, and moved to Chicago as an infant. His adventuresome father, Captain Hannibal Dillingham Pierce, of Maine, met his mother, a prairie schoolteacher named Margretta Moore, when he was shipwrecked along the shores of Lake Michigan and taken in by her family.

Charlie's parents and his uncle Will Moore planned to move to Florida in hopes of curing Moore's tuberculosis, a disease that had killed several of Margretta's other siblings. After the great Chicago Fire of 1871 destroyed every boat in the Chicago boatyard except theirs, the Pierces and Will Moore set sail down the Illinois River in late 1871, only to be frozen in for the winter along the river. After the river thawed, they made their way down the Mississippi River and across the Gulf of Mexico to Cedar Key, on the west coast of Florida. There they were advised not to attempt sailing around Florida during hurricane season. Instead, they sold their boat and traveled by train to Jacksonville. From Jacksonville they headed south along Florida's east coast to a point near modern-day Fort Pierce. It is here that the story begins.

For more information about the author, Harvey E. Oyer III, and Charlie Pierce and his adventures, go to

www.TheAdventuresofCharliePierce.com
Become a friend of Charlie Pierce on **Facebook**
Facebook.com/CharliePierceBooks

Table of Contents

One: **Down the River**..11

Two: **Shipwreck!**...16

Three: **Meeting the Seminoles**...24

Four: **Tiger Bowlegs**...34

Five: **A Lost Rifle Is Found**..40

Six: **Hurricane!**...48

Seven: **Looking for a Home**...60

Eight: **Our House on Hypoluxo Island**...............................68

Nine: **A Christmas to Remember**...74

Ten: **Orange Grove House of Refuge**..................................81

Eleven: **The "Big Rain"**..90

Twelve: *Our Lady of Santa Marta*..97

Chapter One

Down the River

Mama and Papa were in the orange grove pruning tree branches as the midmorning sun rose and heated their backs. I followed close behind, picking up fallen oranges and loading them in a heavy burlap sack. The bumblebees were hard at work, too, flying from orange blossom to orange blossom. I reached up to swat away a bumblebee near my head when Mama shrieked. I thought she had been stung by one of the swarming bees. But to my horror, she was pointing across the grove toward the black smoke billowing from the roof of our old wooden house.

Papa ran as fast as he could toward the house, grabbing a shovel and a bucket of water from near the outhouse. Mama raced behind him so quickly that she almost passed him. Together, they tried to extinguish the raging inferno with buckets of water. But Mama and Papa could not refill the bucket at the pond, get across the yard, and throw the water onto

the fire fast enough. Papa tried shoveling sand onto the fire to smother it. They knew their efforts were hopeless, but they kept fighting anyway. After all, this house and the few meager possessions inside were all we had.

The house was made of a type of pinewood that contained natural oils. I didn't know much about the Florida woods yet, and Papa later told me these oils were very flammable. Once a fire started with this kind of wood, there was almost no chance of putting it out. The Seminole Indians who lived nearby called this type of pine "lighterwood." They used it to start their campfires and cooking fires.

We had just moved into the house a month ago. It was two stories tall with a wraparound porch on the first floor. The wood floors creaked, and strips of peeling paint hung from the walls. The house and the orange grove had been abandoned when we found them. Mama and Papa had spent a month cleaning and repairing the house and trying to restore the orange grove so that it would be productive again.

Now the house was gone. In what seemed like an instant, we went from having a house and a future to having nothing at all. All our clothes and possessions were gone. Not that I had many possessions—only a couple changes of clothes, three books, and a model wooden sailboat.

Papa was very upset. After all, he had convinced Mama to move from the big city of Chicago to this wilderness frontier in Florida.

We had no neighbors and no friends here. In fact, other than a few Seminole Indians, there were no other people within fifty miles.

We did not talk much to the Seminoles. A few years ago, a band of Seminoles had massacred a family of white settlers near here as revenge for a white settler's shooting a Seminole boy. After that, all the other white settlers moved away. That is probably why our house had been abandoned.

I know Papa felt like he had let us down. My mama and I, only eight years old, were going to have to sleep on the ground. We had no house, no food, no clothes, and no idea how we were going to make ends meet. But Mama didn't let Papa stew on it for long.

"Don't worry," she said. "God will provide for us." I believed her.

After all, we hadn't spent a year sailing down the Mississippi River, crossing the Gulf of Mexico, and trekking down the east coast of Florida to give up now. Both Mama and Papa had come from big, wealthy families in the North. Papa was even related to President Franklin Pierce, and Mama had been a schoolteacher. I knew Mama's family was worried about her moving into the jungle because they sent down boxes of books and magazines whenever they could so we would have something to read. Schooling was very important in my house, and Mama was teaching me how to read and write.

By early afternoon, the house was a

smoldering pile of ashes. Only the stone fireplace and part of a charred chimney remained.

It was going to be hot. All the morning dew had already evaporated, and waves of heat were rising from the ground. I played with my shoelaces while Papa paced nervously at the edge of the grove.

Toooot! Toooot!

Two toots of the air horn meant the steamboat was approaching on the river. Our house, or what was left of it, sat on the west bank of the Indian River, just south of Fort Pierce. Twice a week, a small steamboat delivered mail, news from the outside world, and any food that we had ordered from Mr. Titus's store upriver at Sand Point. The steamer was coming from the south, heading back to Sand Point.

Papa waved the steamer down and told Captain Brevard what had happened. Captain Brevard looked over the ruin of our house and then said, "Well, I just came from the Jupiter Lighthouse downriver about forty miles. They need a new assistant lighthouse keeper if you're interested."

"Can you take us?" Papa asked immediately.

Captain Brevard agreed. Soon he had turned his boat around, and we were all headed down the Indian River, leaving behind the smoldering pile of ash that had been our house. We grabbed what few possessions we had left and set off for a brighter future.

Chapter Two

Shipwreck!

We had a fair wind at our backs and made good time down the river. It was October 1872, and the heavy rains from last summer had raised the water level of the Indian River so that Captain Brevard could safely get his boat downriver. During the drier times of the year, some parts of the river became too shallow to cross.

We reached the Jupiter Lighthouse before nightfall. The lighthouse is located at the intersection of three bodies of water: the Indian River, the Loxahatchee River, and the Atlantic Ocean. I later found out that *loxahatchee* means "river of turtles" in the Seminole language.

As we docked, Captain Armour and his assistant, Charles Carlin, were waiting at the end of the long wooden dock. The tall lighthouse rose behind them. I had never seen a lighthouse up close before, but I knew lighthouses were very important because they helped ship captains see where the shore was so they could avoid wrecking. Captain Armour was the lighthouse keeper, and Mr. Carlin was his assistant, but it took three men to operate a lighthouse. After we docked, Papa went ashore to talk to Captain Armour, who said his other assistant had died of yellow fever several weeks ago. He hired Papa on the spot, and we moved right into a small set of rooms above Captain Armour's house. We felt very fortunate to have found a new job and home on the same day we lost our house to fire. Mama was right. God had provided for us.

At first, life at the Jupiter Lighthouse was only a little less lonely than life at the orange grove. Mama and I kept up with our lessons every day. I was quickly becoming a good reader, and my books kept me company. But I also wanted to explore the jungles around the lighthouse. Papa and Captain Armour told me the forest and streams were full of bears, snakes, alligators, and Seminole Indians. Captain Armour didn't seem very interested in exploring, and Papa was busy most of the time. I was desperate to get into the woods, but there was only one other kid around, and she wasn't allowed to explore. Her name was Kate. She was Captain Armour's daughter. We went fishing and swimming every day, but Kate's parents wouldn't let her out of their sight. There were plenty of stories about people getting bitten by gators or snakes, and her parents worried that she would get hurt.

Papa took turns minding the lighthouse with Captain Armour and Mr. Carlin. They

divided each day into three eight-hour shifts. Each man worked one eight-hour shift per day. When Papa was working, I was not supposed to bother him. He had to keep all the lenses and mirrors at the top of the lighthouse clean and working. At night, he carried buckets of oil up the narrow, winding stairs of the lighthouse. The oil was burned to create the light that was then magnified by the lenses and flashed out to sea to tell passing ships where the shoreline was so the ships would not run aground in the middle of the night. Without the lighthouse, Papa said, ships would wreck offshore, and people could get hurt.

We were glad for a place to live, but we still didn't have any possessions or clothes. Mama borrowed a few clothes from Captain Armour's wife for us to wear whenever she washed our one set of clothes. While we were getting used to our new home, I watched Mama carefully to see if I should be worried. I knew Papa was trying his hardest, but I also knew from Mama that sometimes Papa was willing to take big risks. Just moving here had been risky. I figured as long as Mama wasn't worried, then I shouldn't be either.

During the day she seemed fine, and she often said, "God will provide for us, Charlie. Don't you worry about a thing." But one night I was having trouble sleeping, and I heard Mama quietly praying in her room. "Dear Lord," she said, "My family has been through so much, and I know I shouldn't ask for this, because you will provide as you see fit for us, but please, Lord, we have no clothes and nothing of our own. I ask only that my son Charlie is given what he needs to prosper in this foreign land. Thank you, Lord, and amen." Now I knew she was really worried but was hiding it. I decided right then that I wouldn't let Mama down—I would be strong too. Then I fell asleep.

I woke up in the middle of the night, while it was still very dark, and heard Papa climbing down from the top of the lighthouse. I could hear a roaring sound, and for a second, I was scared another fire had started in the lighthouse. Then I realized it was the wind outside. Papa banged on Captain Armour's door below. The captain sounded annoyed when he answered.

"I think there's a ship on the reef," Papa said.

"No," said Captain Armour. "It's too dark outside, too overcast, to see all the way to the reef. There's no ship out there. Now let me get back to sleep."

I heard Papa climb back up to the top of the lighthouse. It seemed like a few minutes later when I woke up again and heard Papa banging on Captain Armour's door. "What now?" Captain Armour said.

"I'm sure of it!" Papa exclaimed excitedly. "There's a ship out there!"

Papa and Captain Armour climbed to the top of the lighthouse to look out, and just minutes later, there was a lot of noise as they ran down the stairs and woke up Mr. Carlin. "There's a ship on the reef!" Captain Armour said. "We need to sail for it and see if they need help!" Mr. Carlin took watch of the lighthouse while Papa and Captain Armour rushed outside into the dark night and rigged out Captain Armour's small sailboat. I desperately wanted to go with them, but I knew I wasn't supposed to be awake, so I didn't even ask.

I watched from the small window in my room while Papa and Captain Armour sailed across the river and to the inlet. I could see their white sail bobbing in the waves, and there were big breakers coming into the mouth of the river. I strained my eyes to see the ship on the reef, but all I could see was black ocean and the white foam from big waves. Eventually, when I couldn't see anything else, I went back to bed.

I was too excited to sleep in and woke up at the first light of dawn. Mr. Carlin was already out on the dock, rigging out his own small sailboat to head out into the surf. In the daylight, I could see how big the waves really were. I had seen big storms in Chicago, on Lake Michigan, but these were the biggest waves I had ever seen. I could also see the ship sitting out on the reef. Huge waves smashed against it, sending white sheets of spray over the rails and deck. I couldn't believe Papa and Captain Armour had sailed into these waves in the middle of the night! I ran outside, passing Mama on the way. "Charlie!" she yelled after me. "You need to eat something!"

21

I could tell she was worried, too, from the way she kept glancing out the window to the inlet. Papa and Captain Armour still hadn't returned from the ship.

"Is Papa going to be all right?" I asked her.

"Of course he is," she said. "Now don't you talk about it anymore."

As soon as I was finished with breakfast, I ran outside and down toward the water. By now, Mr. Carlin was already gone, and the dock was empty. But there was something else there. I looked to the southwest, to where the Lake Worth Creek empties into the Loxahatchee River. I saw a long canoe coming out of the creek and heading toward the lighthouse. Then I saw a second canoe and a third. They kept coming, one after another, until I counted seven canoes, filled with Seminoles, headed directly toward us. Suddenly, everything Captain Armour had said about the Seminoles went through my mind, and I remembered how they had massacred that other white family up in Fort Pierce. I ran back to the house, yelling, "Mama, Mama! The Indians are coming for us!" Mrs. Armour panicked and cried out, "Oh, I wish the men were here!"

Just then, we looked in the other direction, toward the inlet, and saw Papa, Captain Armour, and Mr. Carlin sailing Mr. Carlin's small boat toward us. It was a race. Who would reach us first, Papa and his colleagues or the seven canoes of Indians?

Papa and the other men had the wind and tide in their favor, which meant that the Seminoles were rowing against both. The Seminoles paddled as hard as they could, but it soon became clear that Papa, Captain Armour and Mr. Carlin would reach the dock before the Indians could. Sure enough, Papa, Captain Armour, and Mr. Carlin touched the end of the dock just before the first canoe of Seminoles.

The three men from the lighthouse were not alone in their small sailboat. They brought with them a man, two women, and a child, all huddled under some blankets. They were passengers from the ship on the reef. The ship was named the *Victor* and had set sail from New York toward New Orleans. In the middle of the night, the rudder broke, and the captain could no longer steer the boat. The strong southeast wind pushed the boat onto the reef outside the Jupiter Inlet. Papa, Captain Armour, and Mr. Carlin had helped rescue the passengers from the ship before the ship broke apart in the crashing waves. The crew of the ship stayed behind on the beach.

Now, the three lighthouse keepers, plus the people from the *Victor*, joined me and Mama on the dock, watching the canoes full of Seminoles gliding silently toward us.

Chapter Three

Meeting the Seminoles

As soon as they touched the dock, the Seminole Indians leaped from their canoes and stood facing us on the dock. I was surprised to see the group wasn't just Seminole warriors. They had also brought their wives, whom they called *taykis*, and their children, whom they called *yaatooches*.

This was the first time I'd ever seen Indians up close, and even though Mama always said it was rude to stare, I couldn't help myself. Anyway,

I noticed that the adults were also staring, and Captain Armour looked angry. Mama wrapped her arm around me and pulled me close while the group from the *Victor* stood back and huddled together. They had never seen Indians before either. I felt a heavy hand fall on my shoulder and looked up to see Papa. He didn't look scared or angry, just curious. He winked at me.

The Seminoles wore very colorful clothing that covered them from head to toe. I could see only the dark, smooth skin of their faces and hands. Their eyes were very dark. The Seminoles were not tall like Papa, but their faces looked worn and tough. They did not smile much.

"What do you want here?" Captain Armour demanded.

One of the men stepped forward and looked Captain Armour in the eye. I learned later that Seminoles always stare straight into your eyes when they're talking. "The ship," he said. "We heard ship stuck on reef."

The people from the *Victor* rustled, and the man started to say something. But Captain Armour held up his hand for silence. The taykis and yaatooches watched without expressions on their dark faces. "So there is," said Captain Armour. "But she's still riding the reef. It'll be a few days at least."

The Indian nodded, and it seemed that he and Captain Armour had just made some kind of agreement, but I didn't know what it was. "Fine," the Seminole said. "We will camp upriver."

As he turned to leave, I noticed a boy about my own age standing just behind him. The boy was a little shorter than me, and he was standing all alone with his chin sticking out fiercely. Suddenly, I felt embarrassed because Mama was still holding me, and I squirmed out of her hold and stared back at the boy. He was dressed like the adults, in

25

long pants that went to his ankles, and his feet were bare. He had a necklace around his neck with some kind of bone hanging from it, and he had light streaks in his hair. He seemed just as interested in me as I was in him, and while the rest of his people climbed into canoes, he took a few steps forward, toward me. I noticed then that his legs were a little curved out.

I wanted to back away and hide behind Mama. After all, I knew that Indians killed white people all the time. Everyone knew about it. But I also didn't want to look scared.

When he got within a few steps of me, he stopped and smiled, then stuck out his hand as if he wanted to shake hands. Behind me, I heard Papa whisper, "Well, I'll be darned. Look at that."

That made me feel very brave, so I extended my hand and shook the boy's hand. In very broken English, he said "I am called Tiger Bowlegs."

"I'm Charlie Pierce," I answered.

Tiger looked out to the ocean, where the *Victor* was still being soaked with spray. "You sail on ship?"

"No," I said. "I live here. In the lighthouse."

He nodded. "Very tall."

"Yeah, but it's boring most of the time. Nothing to do around here."

Tiger smiled at me. "Plenty to do. Maybe I show you."

I don't even remember what I answered because I was so excited. Just a year ago, I'd been sitting in my classroom in Chicago, and now I was in the wilds of South Florida talking about exploring the jungles with a real Indian!

Suddenly, I heard an Indian man call out, "Tiger! Come!" Tiger left right away and climbed into a canoe with a group of Seminoles.

Within a few minutes, the whole group of Seminoles was back in their canoes and headed toward the Lake Worth Creek. But they did not go back to the Everglades, where they lived. Instead, they camped for the next two nights along the banks of the Lake Worth Creek. I could see the smoke from their campfire.

Two more days of strong winds and rough seas followed. Each pounding wave did more damage to the *Victor*. There was no chance of getting it off the reef. Every day Captain Armour and Papa sailed out to check on the ship, and every day a canoe full of Seminoles paddled into the river mouth to watch. They were all waiting for the ship to break apart.

Finally, on the third day, the first planks from the *Victor* began to float up on the beach. Captain Armour and Mr. Carlin took a boat across the river to the inlet to collect the goods washing up on the beach while Papa did lighthouse duty.

At about noon a strong incoming tide began pulling all the goods through the inlet toward the lighthouse. I hollered for Papa, who was eating lunch. He dropped his knife and fork and ran to the end of the dock.

Jumping in the other boat, Papa headed into the river to grab as many of the items as he could. There were barrels and boxes of all shapes and sizes going in every direction. Two large boxes were grounded near the dock. Papa left those two alone, knowing that they would not float any farther. All the items were being washed toward the Lake Worth Creek, toward the Seminoles' camp. This was the event they had waited for patiently, and they were coming into the river again in their canoes.

Two Seminoles almost had a large trunk in their canoe when Papa pulled alongside their canoe and yelled, "Stop! That one is mine!" The Seminoles did not argue; they simply let the trunk go. There were so many boxes and barrels in the river that it was not worth arguing over any of them. Papa knew what was in the trunk from the writing on the side. It was a Wheeler and Wilson sewing machine. The Seminoles would have no use for it. Papa got it in his boat, and Mama used it for many years thereafter.

Papa filled his small boat with boxes and trunks so heavy they nearly sank his boat before he could get back to the dock. Every Seminole filled his canoe, too, and there were still more boxes slowly floating up the Loxahatchee River

and the Lake Worth Creek. The wreck of the *Victor* was a bonanza for everyone.

Papa returned with ten one-hundred-pound barrels of butter, which the three families shared for more than a year by soaking the unused butter in brine and burying the barrels in the sand until more butter was needed. More important to Mama and me, one of the two large trunks near the end of the dock contained fifty brand-new men's suits, and the other box contained reams of fine white linen. Mama's prayer had been answered. We now had clothes. In fact, we had more and nicer clothes than we had ever had in our lives. With the sewing machine, Mama was able to alter the men's suits and make new outfits from the linen. We dressed like kings.

Many boxes of what Papa called Plantation Bitters were also recovered, and many more floated upriver. Plantation Bitters was a drink that contained a lot of whiskey and was bottled in one-quart bottles that looked like small log cabins. Papa, Mr. Carlin, and Captain Armour stored the boxes of Plantation Bitters in the storehouse and drank them with moderation.

The Seminoles also recovered many boxes of Plantation Bitters. On one occasion, in the middle of the night, Big Tommy, who was the largest and fiercest of the Seminoles, wandered up to the lighthouse and demanded that we give him our Plantation Bitters. I think he must have been drunk. Captain Armour, who was not a big man, looked Big Tommy in the eye and said, "We no have wyomie (whiskey). Go back to camp, Big Tommy." After asking a few more times and receiving the same answer from Captain Armour, Big Tommy reluctantly got back in his canoe, lay down, and began singing. His melody became fainter and fainter as his canoe drifted back upriver.

Not long afterward, a couple of white men we had never seen before came downriver to the lighthouse. They had stopped at the Seminole village and drunk Plantation Bitters with the Indians the day before. One of the Seminoles, named Charlie Cypress, told the white men that Big Tommy had been one of the band of Seminoles who killed a white family at Mosquito Lagoon a few years back. When the other Seminoles learned that Charlie Cypress had told white men this secret, they were angry at Charlie Cypress but also very scared of what the white men might do. Sometimes the U.S. Army was called in to deal with Indians who killed white people. They might arrest Big Tommy.

Several days later, a canoe with four Seminole village elders arrived at the lighthouse. The elders wanted to talk to Captain Armour. They begged Armour not to report Big Tommy or the other Seminoles to the "Big Chief" in Washington. They didn't want the Army to attack their villages or take Big Tommy away. They admitted the story was true but said, "Many moons have passed. White man and Indians now friends. No want fight anymore. Please, no tell Big Chief in Washington." Captain Armour told the elders that he would not report them to Washington and that the Seminoles and white men were now friends. He had to repeat it many times before the Seminole elders believed him. Eventually, the elders departed in their canoes. After almost forty-two years of war between the Seminoles and the white men, there would never be any fighting between them again.

The elders returned to their village and held a tribal council. They sentenced Charlie Cypress to exile from the village for telling the Big Tommy story to white men. Charlie Cypress was banished from the village for the remainder of his life. He also had one of his ear lobes cut off as a mark of dishonor. He lived alone in the woods for the rest of his days and was known to the settlers as Crop-Eared Charlie.

Chapter Four

Tiger Bowlegs

Life got a lot better after the *Victor*, but it wasn't because of my new clothes or even the sewing machine that Papa fished out of the river. It was because of Tiger Bowlegs. A few days after the *Victor* came apart, I was playing outside by the lighthouse when I heard a short whistle from the trees by the riverbank. At first I thought it was a bird, but then I heard it again. I walked toward the trees and saw Tiger Bowlegs hiding in the shadow of a big oak tree and waving to me. I ran into the woods.

It was hard talking to Tiger at first. I didn't understand him very well, so we both had to talk real slow. I asked why he was hiding in the woods, and he said he was afraid to come out where the white men could see him. I tried to tell him that he didn't have anything to worry about from Papa, Mr. Carlin, and Captain Armour, but he said that Seminoles had been tricked plenty of times by white men. Tiger said the U.S. Army had once burned his family's banana trees and their fields of corn. This happened when the lighthouse we lived in was being built. In revenge, his grandfather led an attack against the workers at the lighthouse and the Army soldiers. This started a war between his tribe and the U.S. Army. It was later called the Third Seminole War.

"What happened? Did you win?" I asked.

Tiger looked fierce and stuck out his chin, but he said, "No. Seminole never win white man fighting."

"Why not?"

"Too many guns."

Tiger told me that Seminoles and white men had been fighting on and off for many years, since before the time of his "father's father's father." It took me a few minutes to figure that out. He meant his great-grandfather. But Seminoles didn't really keep track of time like we do. They followed moons instead of years, so Tiger didn't even know how old he was in years. I just guessed he was somewhere around my age.

I didn't like the idea of white people fighting Indians, and Tiger said that sometimes whole years would go by and there would be no fighting. But then something would happen, like Big Tommy killing the white people or the Army burning a Seminole village, and then there would be a lot of killing.

"Are you going to kill me?" I asked, mostly joking.

Tiger laughed. "No. You my friend."

I saw Tiger pretty often after that. He and his father came to the lighthouse to trade buckskins, bear pelts, and raccoon hides for items such as clothing, tools, and various foods.

One time, Papa let me come along to Tiger's village to get a load of furs. This was the first time I had seen an Indian village, and I couldn't believe how different it was from the houses I was used to. Tiger and his family's house had no walls, and the roof was made from dried palmetto fronds. They slept on a wooden platform a few feet off the ground. He said they did this so animals and snakes could not get them while they slept. In the middle of the village was another big house with a fire pit in the center, where everyone cooked.

Once Mama and Papa learned to trust Tiger, they let us roam through the woods around the lighthouse. We explored the many creeks and little rivers flowing into the Loxahatchee and Indian rivers. We camped, climbed trees, used wild vines to swing from tree to tree, built forts in the woods, hunted rabbits, collected alligator eggs, and learned to make turkey calls that were so good that even the turkeys were confused.

Tiger knew the woods, the river, and the animals better than any white man did. He taught me to hunt, how to move through the woods without making any noise, and how to mask the human smell of my body with mud and plants so the deer could not smell us. He also taught me how to carve crabwood into perfectly straight spears. He then showed me how to crawl out on the edges of mangrove tree branches without casting a shadow over the water. From there, we could spear the fish in the river as they swam below us.

Mama said it was OK if I played with Tiger, but she also said she wasn't going to let me "turn into a little Indian." Every day, I had to sit with her in the lighthouse and study my books and learn to write. But Mama was smart. To keep me interested, she had her relatives in Chicago send books on geography, biology, and plants and animals. So while Tiger taught me the Seminole words for alligator and turtle and river, I also learned the school words for the same things, and even the Latin words. One day Papa walked in during a lesson. He laughed a big laugh and said I was going to "think like a white man but live like a Seminole." That was one thing about Papa. He never said anything bad about the Seminoles, and he was friendly toward Tiger and his father. He told me the Seminoles knew how to live with the land, not against it, and he said I was lucky to learn from a real Indian.

I spent as much time with Tiger as I could. One of our favorite places was the large shell mountain on the other side of the inlet from the lighthouse. It was a big hill made from old oyster shells, along with bones, arrowheads, burnt wood, broken turtle shells, and axe heads. We liked to climb to the top and look out over

the trees and water. Tiger taught me how to weave green palmetto fronds into mats so we could slide from the top of the shell mountain all the way to the bottom. If it had just rained and the shells were slippery, we had to jump off our mats before plunging into the river.

Tiger's father told us that the shell mountain was once the home of a group of Indians who called themselves *Hobe*. The shells, bones, and tools belonged to the Hobe, who lived here long before the Seminoles arrived. According to Tiger's father, the Hobe had kept a white man named Jonathan Dickinson and his family captive at this site after Mr. Dickinson's ship had wrecked north of the inlet. It took Dickinson and his family more than a year to escape and walk north along the beach to St. Augustine. If only the people on board the *Victor* knew how lucky they were to be rescued by Papa, Mr. Carlin, and Captain Armour rather than a band of wild Indians. About twenty-five years after my family moved away from the lighthouse, a family named DuBois would build a large house on top of that shell mountain.

Chapter Five

A Lost Rifle Is Found

Even though the fighting between the Seminoles and the white men was over, there were still plenty of reminders of what happened. Just a little ways away from our lighthouse, a point of land stuck into the Loxahatchee River. There was an old, abandoned fort on this land. Captain Armour said the fort used to be called Fort Jupiter. The Seminoles and the U.S. Army had fought over the fort a long time before the lighthouse was even built. Tiger knew about the fort, too, because his grandfather had actually attacked it during the Second Seminole War.

Because the fort had been made of wood and because of the extreme humidity, the fort was mostly destroyed. In Florida, winter was almost like summer in Chicago, and the weather was nice almost every day. But by April, Mama was already complaining about the heat, and the grown-up men wore loose shirts or no shirts at all and sweated all day, every day. Pretty soon, the rains started, and I learned what Captain Armour meant when he said that summer in Florida is like being a lobster in a pot. It was very, very hot, and it rained almost every day in the late afternoon.

Tiger never seemed bothered by the heat. He thought it was funny when he saw Papa with a red face and sweat rolling down his neck. He said Indians weren't bothered by the heat.

Papa and Mr. Carlin also complained because the heat and the dampness destroyed wood so fast, they had to constantly repair the house. The lighthouse was fine because it was made from brick. Because no one was fixing the old fort, however, it was mostly ruined. Much of it had fallen down, the roof had caved in,

and the rotten walls were full of animals and all kinds of huge bugs. But I thought it was the best place to play anywhere around. Tiger and I spent whole afternoons pretending to attack and defend the fort. I was usually a U.S. Army officer, and he played his grandfather, who actually did attack the fort many moons ago. Tiger was good at this game. Seminoles can move through the forest without making any sound at all, and he snuck up on me all the time. We tried to switch our roles a few times, but it didn't work. I was too loud to be a Seminole, and Tiger didn't like playing a U.S. Army officer. He said it made him unhappy to pretend to kill Seminoles.

When we weren't in the fort, we sometimes went exploring up the river. Tiger had his own small canoe. His father made it for him out of a log of cypress wood that he hollowed out. Tiger taught me how to sit in the middle and paddle so the canoe wouldn't flip over, and we would glide down the river, pretending to shoot alligators and looking for herons or snook.

One day, we went farther up the river than we ever had before. The oak trees were growing close to the river, and the branches wore Spanish moss like beards.

"Listen," Tiger said.

"I don't hear anything except wind."

"Yes." He told me we were near a haunted place where the wind talked to people. He said it was haunted because "many white man and Seminoles died here." It was an old battlefield from the Seminole wars. He looked nervous because his father had told him never to go to this place.

The area was like no other place I had ever seen. The river narrowed and weaved through beautiful oak hammocks that hung over the river. We found a spot along the river to wedge the canoe so it couldn't float away. Then we climbed up the river bank and walked through the beautiful forest of ancient oak trees. Unlike the fort, which still had walls, cisterns, and wells, the battlefield site was just a grassy meadow.

We walked slowly through the haunted forest. "Look!" I said, bending over to pick up a used bullet. It turned out the ground was littered with things left over from the battle. We found used bullets, U.S. Army belt buckles, arrowheads, and metal buttons that must have been attached to military uniforms that had long since disintegrated.

Pretty soon we found our first skeleton, half buried under leaves. Tiger and I stood in silence, staring at it. I'd never seen a skeleton before. It looked so small. Overhead, the wind rattled in the oak trees, and I wondered whether the old battlefield really was haunted. There were scraps of clothing still hanging from the mossy old bones, and Tiger pointed silently to an arrowhead lodged in a rib. "Soldier," he whispered, his eyes wide.

After that, we found a lot more skeletons. A few of them had bullet holes in their skulls where they had been shot. These were dead Seminoles, and I felt bad for Tiger because he said that some of these warriors might have been in his tribe a long time ago. Later, I learned that we had found the graveyard of the greatest battle of the Second Seminole War. The battle occurred in January 1838.

Tiger and I didn't talk hardly at all. He was afraid of upsetting the spirits, and I was daydreaming. It seemed as if I could even hear the sounds of the battle in the forest around me. I stared into the treetops, trying to understand what the voices were saying. Tiger's father said you had to listen closely to understand the language of the winds.

WHAP!

I snapped out of it when I walked straight into the biggest oak tree I'd ever seen and fell down. I got back up and brushed myself off, then checked my cheek to see if I was bleeding. I wasn't. I couldn't believe I didn't see the tree. Its trunk was almost as big around as the lighthouse. The bottom of the trunk was hollow and big enough for a grown man to stand up inside.

I was afraid there might be a bear or snakes or some other critter inside the trunk, so I only put my head in slowly. After my eyes adjusted to the darkness, I saw something glitter in one corner. I squinted to see it, but it was all the way at the back of the trunk. I was afraid to walk into the darkness. If I got bit by a snake or attacked by a bear, I didn't want Tiger to have to explain how I died in the one place his father told us never to go.

Then I remembered that I had some matches wrapped in a burlap cloth in my back pocket. I removed a match and struck it on the bark of the tree. There were no animals inside. There was nothing inside except a gleaming, perfectly preserved rifle leaning against one side of the trunk. Just as the flame of the match reached my fingers, I grabbed the rifle and ran out of the tree trunk.

I yelled for Tiger, and he came running from somewhere deep in the forest.

"What?"

"Look!" I held the rifle up so he could see it. This was no standard-issue Army rifle. The stock and barrel were engraved with elaborate designs. Engraved on the butt of the rifle was a man's name: "Major William Lauderdale."

"Who that?" Tiger said.

"I don't know. It sounds familiar, but I don't know who it is."

Tiger grunted. "We go now," he said. I think he wasn't comfortable about the rifle, or maybe he was just worried his father might find out he had been at the battlefield. If Tiger's father found out, Tiger would never be allowed to play with me again. I took the rifle back to the canoe without even thinking about how I would explain to Papa where it came from. But I couldn't leave it behind. It was the nicest rifle I had ever seen, and rifles were expensive.

Back at the lighthouse, I told Papa the truth about where the rifle came from. He agreed not to tell Tiger's father where we had been. But I knew Papa was unhappy with me for helping Tiger disobey his father. Tiger and I never returned to the battlefield site again.

Captain Armour recognized the name William Lauderdale right away. He said that Lauderdale was the officer who commanded a group of soldiers called the Tennessee

Volunteers at the battle thirty-five years ago. He became famous, and a fort farther down the coast was later named for him. Some years later, when I was an adult, I traveled many times to Fort Lauderdale.

After we sanded some rust off it and oiled the firing pin, the rifle worked perfectly. Papa kept a watchful eye on my use of it until I got a little older. When I was a teenager, though, I used it almost every day. I kept the rifle for the rest of my life. While I would own other rifles during my lifetime, none ever fired as true, straight, and far as Ol' Lauderdale.

Chapter Six

Hurricane!

I liked the lighthouse, but I knew we wouldn't be staying there forever. It was because of Papa. I heard him say often enough that he was an adventurer, and he often said he had no intention of living out his days in a lighthouse.

But living at the lighthouse sounded pretty good to me—especially because I didn't know what else we would do. Whenever I complained to Mama that I didn't want to move and that I liked the lighthouse, she always smiled and said, "Yes, but that's not how your Papa lives." She said that as if it was a good thing.

Mama meant that Papa was an adventurer. My Papa came from wealthy, well-educated people in New England, but he had run away from home when he was sixteen to find excitement. As a teenager, he sailed on clipper ships around the world. He lived in Australia during the gold rush of the 1840s, saw pygmies in Papua New Guinea, was shipwrecked in the Florida Keys in the 1860s, was a scout in the Blackhawk Indian Wars, and was an officer in the Union Army in the American Civil War. In fact, he met Mama only because he was shipwrecked on the shores of Lake Michigan after a terrible storm. Mama's parents took him in after the storm, and he fell in love with their daughter.

So when a few men showed up at the lighthouse and started talking about Lake Worth, to the south of us, I knew something was about to happen because I saw Papa get excited. Papa kept them at the dinner table one night until very late, asking all kinds of questions. "What's the water like?" "Are there turkeys in the woods?" "How are the Indians down there?"

I knew I shouldn't be listening, but I couldn't help it. I slipped out of bed and crept to the door so I could hear. The men told Papa that Lake Worth was like a paradise. They said the water was clear and warm and filled with fish and oysters. The woods were full to bursting with wild turkey, deer, and other game. Better yet, one of the men said the government was giving land away for free. It was called homesteading, and it meant that if a man filed a claim with the State Land Office in Gainesville, he could have 160 acres of land as long as he agreed to live on it.

The next day at breakfast, Papa set down his fork and smiled at me. He was smiling, but he looked serious at the same time. I got nervous. "Charlie," he said, "those men yesterday told me about a place just to the south of here where we can build a real home on a big lake and live on our own land. It's called Lake Worth, and we're going to move there."

Mama was watching me closely, too. I had to act surprised at first, as if I did not already know, because I had been eavesdropping. But the truth was, I was angry. I didn't want to leave. I liked Captain Armour and Kate and Mr. Carlin, but most of all, I liked Tiger Bowlegs. From what Papa said, there weren't any kids down at Lake Worth. From what he said, there wasn't anybody at all down there. And he said that as if it was a good thing.

Then it got even worse. Papa said he wouldn't be getting his $33 per month salary anymore for working at the lighthouse, so we would have to get by on hunting, fishing, farming, and salvaging items from the occasional shipwreck. We were truly going to be pioneer settlers on the lake.

I didn't say much about his plans. Secretly, I hoped they wouldn't work out.

But things moved pretty fast after that. When I told Tiger we would be moving to Lake Worth, he looked sad. He said that his family almost never went that far south, so we probably wouldn't see each other much after I moved.

Meanwhile, Mama and Papa started getting ready for the big move. The year before, Papa

50

had salvaged the lifeboat from the wreck of the *Victor*. He rigged it with a set of sails and named it *Victor II*, in honor of its destroyed mother ship. The *Victor II* was not a good sailing vessel. It had been built as a lifeboat, with no centerboard and no deep keel. Papa also built a twelve-foot-long skiff from white pine lumber salvaged from the wreck. This would be the tender boat to the *Victor II*.

Papa's plan was to sail the *Victor II* west along the Loxahatchee River to the Lake Worth Creek and then to the top of Lake Worth. On the day that we left, Captain Armour came down to the dock to say good-bye. He looked worried. "Are you sure you know where you're going?" he said, looking up the river to the jungle.

"Sure," said Papa. "It's only about seven miles to the top of Lake Worth. The Indians say there's a passage through the Lake Worth Creek. Can't be that hard to find a way through."

"I don't know," Captain Armour said, looking doubtful. "There's a swamp between here and there. It'd be mighty easy to get lost in a place like that."

But Papa just laughed and slapped me on the shoulder. "We'll be just fine," he said. "After all, little Charlie here is about half Indian by now."

I didn't say anything. I just sat in the bow of our little boat, wishing we didn't have to leave. But too soon, Captain Armour shoved us off from the dock, and they all waved as we sailed west, up the river to join up with the Lake Worth Creek. We sailed the first mile with a pretty good wind and the jungle sliding by on both banks. The air was full of birds and insects, and I strained my eyes to see into the dark trees just in case Tiger Bowlegs was hiding. But he wasn't.

When we hit the Lake Worth Creek, a strong headwind kicked up from the south, pushing us backward. Papa dropped the sails and glanced at the sky. Mama looked up, too. I thought she looked a little nervous, but she didn't say anything.

Now that we couldn't sail anymore, Papa had to row. So he got into the skiff and towed me and Mama, in the *Victor II,* behind him. It was slow, hard work. Papa was soon sweating through his shirt, and I could hear him puffing, even from the *Victor II*. We were able to raise the sails a few times when the river turned west again, but Papa mostly spent that whole afternoon dragging me and Mama and everything we owned up the creek.

Papa's goal was to reach an old Indian campground near the head of the creek, where he said there was a set of rapids that separated the creek from a great swamp of reeds called sawgrass that spread out in every direction. Somewhere on the other side of the sawgrass swamp was the northern edge of Lake Worth. We would have to navigate our way through the sawgrass to find the one and only route that actually reached the lake. The problem was that Papa had never been here before and did not even know the way to the Indian campground, let alone the way through the sawgrass swamp on the other side.

We finally reached the old Indian campground just as the sun was beginning to set. It wasn't a very impressive camp, just a bare dirt hill only a few feet above the waterline and surrounded by thick jungle. But the ground had been cleared by the Indians, and it was dry, so Papa said it was a good place to camp. He said we'd be here for a few days until he figured out how to get through the sawgrass swamp to the lake.

I didn't like living at the camp. It was very hot at night, and there were so many mosquitoes that we could barely sleep. I woke up over and over that first night because of a mosquito buzzing in my ear. I wanted to be back at the lighthouse, in my own bed, so badly that I had to fight to keep from crying.

Mama tried to cheer me up while Papa was gone during the day, but there was almost nothing for us to do. We couldn't explore the jungle because it was too thick to walk through, and we couldn't get too near the water because it was full of alligators. Lots of times, we saw many alligators swim by, and once we saw a reddish snake that must have been four feet long. Mama grabbed me and hissed at me to be quiet. She said it was a very dangerous kind of snake that would kill me if it bit me. I already knew that because Tiger had told me about these kinds of snakes, but I didn't say anything.

Finally, on the third day, Papa came back early from rowing through the narrow channels by the rapids. He sat down heavily on the dirt and mopped sweat from his face.

"Well?" said Mama. "Did you find a way through? I don't know that we can stand much more of this."

Papa sighed. "No. The channels are too narrow for the *Victor II*. I guess we'll just have to row the skiff through and leave the big boat here. You're right. We can't stay here much longer. I'll come back with your brother once we find the lake. He and I will just have to figure out a way to get the *Victor II* to Lake Worth." Uncle Will, Mama's brother, had sailed down the Atlantic coast to meet us at Lake Worth. He was probably already there. I wanted to tell Papa that we should have sailed, too, but I didn't say anything.

The next morning was sunny and very beautiful. Even Papa remarked on it. There wasn't a whisper of wind in the soft air. Mama packed just enough food in the skiff for one meal, and we set off to find a route through the sawgrass. She brought a piece of fat pork, some tea, syrup, and a bottle of cognac that had been salvaged from the safe of the *Victor* shipwreck last year.

It was still early morning when Papa began rowing us through the sawgrass swamp. The sawgrass grew very high, and it looked as if we were going through a tunnel of brown grass. Papa warned me sternly not to grab the giant blades of grass. He said it was called sawgrass for a reason, and I could cut my hand, and there was no doctor anywhere around to fix it.

By afternoon, I was hot and tired, but I was also worried. Mama and Papa weren't paying much attention, but a few times, I had heard animals nearby, running along hidden trails in the swamp. And I had seen flocks of birds flying overhead, straight and fast. They were going west. I didn't know as much as an Indian, but Tiger said the way to know the land was to watch the animals. He said animals and birds knew more about the land than even the Indians and that it was a bad sign whenever you saw an animal do something strange.

"Papa," I finally said, "something is wrong."

He kept rowing. "What are you talking about?"

"What's wrong?" said Mama.

"I don't know," I said. "But the birds are acting funny. Tiger says that when the animals act strange, something is wrong. And they're all acting strange. They're flying too straight and fast."

Mama and Papa looked at each other, and Papa shrugged. "Well, nothing we can do about the birds," he said. "We'll just have to push through. At least we've got some beautiful weather."

Mama nodded and patted my head.

But I was right. Something was wrong. The weather didn't stay beautiful for long. A little while later, we got hit by a thunderstorm. It seemed to come out of nowhere, and we heard it before we saw it. The wind whipped through the sawgrass, and the rain struck the water like a drum. The storm swept over us and soaked everything and blew rain into our faces, and then it went away. By this time, the sky was gray, and there were fast-moving clouds. Mama and Papa both looked worried now, and Mama told me to lie down in the bottom of the skiff just in case another storm came.

"I've never seen a storm like that," Papa said to Mama. "It was moving so fast."

The rest of the afternoon, we kept getting hit with fast-moving storms, and each storm was bigger than the last. The wind and rain started coming constantly, and the air filled with the roar of sawgrass pounding against the water. By late afternoon, the sky was completely black, and water was sloshing around in the bottom of the boat. I was freezing in the strong wind, and even in the small channels, the wind kicked up foamy waves. Papa kept rowing as best he could, but he wasn't making any progress. The wind just pushed us all over the place, and before long, Mama crawled down next to me and wrapped her body around mine to keep me warm and protect me from the bits of flying grass.

"Don't worry, baby," she whispered. "We'll be OK. God will protect us."

By now, we knew it was a hurricane. Papa had told me about hurricanes. He said the number one rule in a hurricane was not to be stuck outside on the water. And that's just where we were. He fought the oars and cursed, and water streamed from his face. I saw him bleeding from a cut on his cheek where a piece of the sharp grass had hit him.

Soon it was night, and the hurricane showed no sign of passing. The situation was desperate. We were nowhere near land, and we could only see a few feet in front of the skiff. Papa had given up trying to push through the river and was now searching for any dry land. His only light was flashing lightning. Finally, he found a gator trail through the sawgrass. The skiff was wider than even the largest gator, so it took all of the energy Papa had left to push the skiff up the gator trail to a mound of wet dirt a few inches above the waterline. This mound of dirt was where gators lay in the sun to warm themselves on sunny days. It would now be our place of refuge during the hurricane.

Papa cleared an opening with his axe. He also cut some palmetto fronds and scattered them on the ground for our beds. It was too wet for a fire, so we ate the fat pork uncooked, together with the syrup. Papa and Mama drank some of the cognac. The wind was now howling out of the southeast. Papa turned the skiff over on top of us to protect us from the hurricane. The wind was so powerful that it lifted the skiff up several times despite Papa

and Mama's holding it down from the inside with all their strength.

I lay on the wet palm fronds and watched my parents fight the storm. Every so often, something would THUD into the boat, probably a log the wind had picked up. I was more scared than I'd ever been. I was afraid that the wind would pick the boat up and blow us away too. Mama and Papa watched each other as they held on. It was too loud to talk or even yell very often, but I could tell they were scared, too.

Finally, believe it or not, my eyes began to close, and I fell asleep in the middle of a howling hurricane, lying under a little wooden skiff that Papa had built from lumber salvaged from the *Victor*. I guess I was able to fall asleep because I was too young and naïve to understand the danger we were in.

Chapter Seven

Looking for a Home

The next morning, I woke up and wondered where I was. Then I realized I was still lying on wet palm fronds on the muddy ground, underneath the upside-down boat. Mama and Papa were both sleeping. Papa had one arm looped over a bench in the little skiff. Mama was curled up on the ground and covered with mud. Her clothes, which had once been white linen and nice fabric from the men's suits, were filthy and ruined. I realized that Mama and Papa must have held the boat almost all night, through the entire storm.

I crawled out from underneath the skiff without waking them up. I stood and looked around in amazement. Birds flew over the swamp, and a cool breeze was blowing in from the northwest. There were a few high clouds, but it was sunny. The sawgrass that had been pounding so loud the night before was standing up and waving in the gentle breeze.

I couldn't believe it. The only sign that a hurricane had passed through was the swamp. The water was stirred up to a deep brown, and bits of leaves and whole branches floated by.

Papa woke up a few minutes later and joined me outside. He looked very tired. His eyes were red, and the cut on his cheek was a big scab. His whiskers were growing out, and his shirt was torn. But he was smiling. "That was some storm, eh, Charlie?" he said.

"Yes, Papa. It sure was."

"Well, now we can say we survived a hurricane. Not many people can say that."

"I guess not."

He thumped on the boat to wake up Mama, then announced it was time for him to leave in the skiff. We were out of food now, and we desperately needed to find a way through the swamp if we wanted to survive. I knew it could get serious if we were lost in the sawgrass. Tiger said that even Indians got lost in the swamp sometimes, and not all of them came back to the village. Mama and I stood on the bank and watched Papa row away again and disappear into the tall sawgrass.

But this time, he came back an hour later with the good news that the mysterious "haulover" area between the swamp and the lake was very near. Even in the rain and dark, we had made our way to the edge of the haulover.

Once we reached the haulover area, we had another problem. The lake was at least three hundred yards from the end of the swamp. The three hundred yards in between were all dry land. How would we haul the skiff over three hundred yards of dry land? The Seminoles cut the wild pawpaw and used the stalks as skids, which they rolled their canoes over. But there was no pawpaw growing nearby. Papa decided to use brute force and just pull the skiff over the dry land. He did it in spurts of twenty or thirty yards at a time. By the time he reached the top of the lake, he was completely exhausted. He had not slept in more than twenty-four hours and had eaten only some uncooked fat pork and syrup the night before.

Mama and I cheered when Papa finally pushed the skiff into the clear waters of Lake Worth. Then we climbed into the boat, and Papa started rowing again. From the water, it was easier to see where the hurricane had destroyed trees, and I saw where one whole tree had been knocked over and was sticking up from the lake. It was filled with big white birds, watching the water below.

I had no idea where we were going, and Papa just kept rowing. I started to get hungry, but when I complained to Mama, she just said, "Hush now. We'll eat soon enough."

"Where?" I asked. "Where are we going?"

"Charlie, just let Papa do his work in peace."

I could tell she was getting nervous again, and I tried to stop my stomach from growling. But it didn't work.

Finally, we saw a house along the shore. Papa pulled the oars into the boat and rested for a minute. He shaded his eyes with his hand. "There it is," he said, grinning. "The Malden house. I was beginning to think we'd never find it and we'd have to eat young Charlie here. He was starting to look pretty meaty to me."

"Hey!" I said, and Mama laughed. Papa was just joking.

I knew Mr. and Mrs. Malden, but not very well. They had visited the lighthouse a few times while we lived there. That's how Papa knew where they lived. Soon enough, we had docked at their tiny dock, and Papa hailed them from the boat. Mr. Malden appeared in the doorway, followed by Mrs. Malden. I saw that their yard was a mess from the hurricane. A big tree had lost most of its branches, and it looked as if Mr. Malden had spent the morning cutting them up with a hand saw and stacking the wood. Mrs. Malden had tied a kerchief around her head and rolled her sleeves up like a man. She had been cleaning the walls of the house.

The Maldens were really nice. They took us in right away, and Mrs. Malden went to the stove to prepare a quick meal. While we ate, they listened to Papa tell the story of hiding underneath the boat while the hurricane passed by. Mr. Malden leaned back in his chair and said, "Well, that's just the most incredible thing I've ever heard. Charlie, your Papa must be the luckiest man on God's green Earth."

I just nodded. I was very hungry, and I didn't see what was so lucky about getting stuck outside in a storm anyway.

We ended up staying with the Maldens for a couple of days while Papa recovered his strength. On the third day, we thanked the Maldens and set off down the lake in search of the best land to make our homestead.

Several miles down the lake, we spotted a small cabin perched high in the overgrown jungle of the barrier island. We landed the skiff nearby and ventured up to the cabin, shouting "Hello! Is anyone home?"

There was nobody. I later found out that the cabin had been built by a German immigrant named Augustus O. Lang. The legend was that Lang was living farther north on the coast of Florida when the American Civil War erupted. Being from Germany, he had no interest in the outcome of an American Civil War, but he was afraid he might get drafted into the Confederate army and sent up north to fight, as had happened to lots of Irishmen who came to this country during that war. So, to avoid fighting in a war he didn't care about, Lang traveled down to South Florida and hid himself in the vast jungles.

He lived alone in this cabin on the barrier island for years, growing his own fruits and vegetables, harvesting fish and oysters, and hunting wild game. As the legend goes, Lang lived so removed from civilization that when the American Civil War ended in 1865, he had no idea that the war was over. After all, there were no newspapers, and no other people lived within miles of his cabin.

In 1866, a family named Sears who lived near Miami, had sailed north to Sand Point to purchase supplies. On their return voyage down the coast, they noticed that heavy rains had broken open a natural inlet into Lake Worth.

They sailed through the inlet to explore Lake Worth. To their great surprise, they found Lang living all alone like a hermit in his cabin. When Lang asked how the war was going, the Sears family told him that it had ended a year earlier. Shortly thereafter, Lang abandoned the cabin and moved north. He had successfully avoided the entire war.

Now we were thinking about moving into Lang's cabin. It wasn't nearly as nice as the lighthouse. The whole cabin was made of lumber that had probably been salvaged from a shipwreck. The roof looked just like a Seminole roof. It was made of dried palmetto fronds. There were a few empty bottles and cans littering the floor, and turtle shells, animal bones, and firewood were scattered around outside.

"Well?" said Papa.

"I don't know…" Mama said. "It's not very well kept, is it? And it's pretty small, with just one room for the three of us."

"Surely," said Papa, "there's not much room for a family here."

Papa looked around a little more, then shook his head. "No," he said. "We can do better than this." So we sailed south once again. The lake was about twenty-five miles long, and we had explored only the first five or so miles. Over the next two days, we sailed all the way to the bottom of the lake, looking for the best place to live.

Chapter Eight

Our House on Hypoluxo Island

You never do things the easy way," Mama said for the tenth time.

"Well, it makes sense to me," Papa answered a little grumpily.

We were standing on a narrow strip of land that Papa had decided should be our new home. It was an island. And, as Mama had pointed out many times, there was no bridge between us and the shore. No one else lived on the island, and as far as we could see, no animals lived here either. "The way I see it," Papa said, "this is the perfect place to put down roots. We're protected by the lake, just in case any bears get it in their minds to pay us a visit, and we'll have plenty of fresh water."

Mama grumbled. "Let's just hope we don't need to go anywhere very fast."

No one asked me, but I thought Papa had

picked a fine spot to live. I liked the idea of living on an island, surrounded by the clear, warm water of Lake Worth. As we'd been sailing down the lake, I'd seen dozens of fish—some almost as big as me—shooting through the water, and there were always flocks of birds flying above.

The island Papa picked was about two-thirds of the way down Lake Worth. He said he wanted to build our house on the highest point on the south end of the island. Uncle Will and his family could build their house on the north end of the island. Uncle Will was supposed to join us a few days later.

We camped out until Uncle Will arrived. He and Papa left right away and returned to Jupiter to bring the *Victor II* back, this time by ocean. Miraculously, all of our possessions in the *Victor II* survived the hurricane relatively undamaged.

When Papa and Uncle Will returned, Papa announced that he was going to start the house. He said he was going to build a "fortress that could survive any hurricane." This he did. Our house stood for almost one hundred years and withstood countless hurricanes.

But it also took a lot of extra work to build a hurricane-proof house. First we had to scavenge lumber and wood from the beach. A hurricane three years earlier had caused many ships to wreck, and their cargoes and pieces of their hulls were strewn for miles up and down the sand. Once we found a piece of wood we liked, we had to drag it, sometimes for miles up the beach, through the jungle, and over the beach ridge, and then raft it across the lake to the island. It took almost three weeks to collect all the wood we needed, and we camped out those three weeks under a tent Uncle Will brought for us.

As we combed the beach looking for lumber, we also found all sorts of useful articles, including bolts, nails, and pieces of copper and brass. This made Papa happy because he could sell the copper and brass by the pound to Mr. Titus, who owned the store at Sand Point. Although almost 120 miles away, it was the nearest store where we could purchase flour, coffee, sugar, and ammunition—which were all essentials.

Papa selected only the very best timbers for our house. The corner posts were ten inches by twelve inches, about triple the size of corner posts on any house in Chicago. The corner posts were the cross beams from ships' hulls and had been treated with some type of tar to prevent water rot and insect infestation. After he got the posts to the island, Papa worked for days to dig into the solid limestone under the topsoil. He dug holes two feet deep, and then he and Uncle Will sunk the corner posts in the stone. They next framed in the walls with timbers that were six inches by nine inches. The wall studs were four inches by four inches, double the size of wall studs used in houses elsewhere.

The roof was a whole different kind of

problem. There were no shingles on the beach, so we had to do what the Seminoles did. We cut and dried palmetto fronds and layered them over each other to create the roof. The palmetto fronds were plentiful and easy to use, but neither me nor Mama liked our new roof very much. The first problem was that the palmetto fronds rotted quickly, and Papa had to replace the roof every two to three years. The other big problem was cockroaches, which were called "palmetto bugs" for a good reason. They liked to live in palmetto fronds. The first time a big, black roach dropped from the ceiling, Mama almost yelled herself hoarse, and I ran screaming from the house. No matter how much time I spent in the woods with Tiger Bowlegs, I never got used to the roaches. And now I had to live with dozens of them in the roof of my house.

Then, one day, I heard Mama shriek, but it wasn't because of another roach. There was a red snake up in the rafters. Papa came running in when he heard her holler, and he laughed when she pointed out the snake. "That's good news," Papa said. "You watch. That snake eats cockroaches. In no time at all, I bet he'll take care of your little bug problem."

Sure enough, in just a few days, roaches stopped dropping from the ceiling, and Mama declared that the little red snake was part of the family. She even named it Orion, after the great hunter in Homer's *Odyssey*. From that point onward, we had much less of a cockroach problem.

Two months after moving onto the island,

we had our first visitors. It was a group of three Seminole men, who appeared in our yard in that strange, silent way that Seminoles have of traveling. One of the Indians hailed Papa. He knew us from the lighthouse. "Pierce," he asked, "what you make?" The Seminole pointed at the hutch Papa was building. A hutch was a special building used to store dry goods like flour and sugar. It was built on raised legs like stilts, and the legs were sunk into buckets of turpentine. The turpentine smelled awful, but bugs like roaches and ants couldn't climb through it, so it protected the dry goods.

"It's a cage to keep my tayki and yaatooches," Papa answered. The three Seminoles looked confused for several moments before they saw Papa's grin and knew that he was only kidding.

The Seminole then asked Papa how long we had been on "Hypoluxo."

"Hypoluxo?" said Papa. "What does that mean?"

One of the Seminoles waved at the lake and said, "Means water all around, no get out."

"Oh," said Papa, shading out the sun with his hand so he could look around the island. "We call it an island. But I like Hypoluxo better. It has a nice ring to it."

From that day forward, we too called it Hypoluxo, as it is known to this day.

Chapter Nine

A Christmas to Remember

Papa and Uncle Will finished the house in early fall, and everybody agreed it was a very strong house. Once the roach problem was fixed, Mama said she was especially happy it was a dry house, too. It rained almost every day in September, but the palmetto roof kept the water out.

Pretty soon, it was almost Christmastime. Back in Chicago, Christmas had been my favorite holiday. We saw Mama's big family,

there were endless desserts and presents, and we went to night services in a big stone church with hundreds of candles. But this year, I was a little worried. We were living all alone on an island, and we hardly ever saw anybody. I couldn't imagine what kind of Christmas we'd have.

Then one day, Papa announced that we had been invited to Mr. Lachlan Reed's house for Christmas. Mr. Reed was a bachelor, which meant he didn't have a wife or kids. I was disappointed to hear that. But Papa said Mr. Reed had moved into Lang's abandoned shack up the lake, and even though he was a bachelor, he wanted our whole family to come over for the holiday. So on Christmas Eve, we packed the *Victor II* and sailed north. We set out the day before Christmas because the trip could take a long time if we did not have a favorable wind at our back. Luckily, we had a good wind from the south, and we made good time.

As was custom in those days, if we visited another person's home, we brought our own bedding mats and mosquito netting so that we could sleep on the floor of the host's home. Lach, as everyone called him, had cleaned Lang's abandoned cabin up nicely. The fruit trees were tended again, and vegetables were growing in the flat areas of the beach ridge.

As soon as we got there, I stuck out my hand to shake hands and said, "It's nice to meet you, Mr. Reed," just like Mama had shown me. But Mr. Reed just laughed and said, "Call me Lach, young man. I think I've got something you might like. Follow me."

He took me back out to the yard and showed me a cage made from bamboo. Inside the cage was the fattest possum I'd ever seen, and I'd seen a lot of fat possums in the woods since moving to Florida. Lach looked at the possum happily. "I caught him nigh on a month ago," he said. "I've been feeding him sweet potatoes ever since. You know what his name is?"

"No, sir."

"I call him Christmas dinner!" Then Lach laughed so hard, I thought I saw him crying a little bit. When we went back inside, he told Mama that he cooked up the best possum of any man alive, and if she were interested, he would show her his own special recipe. Mama didn't seem too thrilled about learning to cook possum, but I'll admit that I was pretty hungry to try some of his roasted Christmas possum.

On Christmas morning, we didn't go to church like we would have done in Chicago. There was no church anywhere around. Instead, Lach went outside and brought the possum cage inside. Papa said a short prayer over the possum, and we all thanked Lach and thanked God for giving us such a wonderful meal on Christmas. Then Lach took the possum back outside, and pretty soon, Christmas dinner was gutted and skewered on a spit that turned slowly over a wood fire.

For once, I had the whole day to myself. No lessons. No chores. Papa and Uncle Will sat with Lach on the tiny porch while Mama busied herself with a little sewing and talking to Lach about food. It turned out that Lach knew almost as much as Mama did about cooking. He said that he even had a recipe for alligator tail that was as good as a fresh young chicken. I wasn't so sure about that, but Tiger Bowlegs had also said that alligator meat was good, so I figured it probably was.

At noontime, we sat around a rickety wooden table and waited while Lach brought over a platter with the roasted possum's paws draped over the sides. I'd been hungry while the possum cooked, but when I saw it on the table, my appetite disappeared. Lach had left the head and legs, even the claws, on the big, fat possum. At least he had taken it off the spit. I saw Mama and Papa looking a little nervous also. But Lach just laughed and picked some meat off the possum. "Trust me," he said.

And he was right. Once we started eating it, Mama declared it was the finest possum she'd ever had. Of course, Mama, like Papa and me, had never had possum before. However, the meat tasted like fresh young pig and was delicious. Mama also made her famous biscuits, which we smothered in fresh cane syrup that had been sent to us by Captain Miles Burnham in Cape Canaveral.

For dessert, we had a prickly pear pie. Prickly pears are the bright red fruit that grows on a cactus. The sandy pinewoods of Hypoluxo Island were covered with cactus, so Mama usually had plenty of prickly pears. The color was bright and beautiful, but the taste was a little boring. I thought prickly pear pie looked a lot better than it actually tasted. Mama usually had to add a lot of sugar to make it good.

After Christmas dinner, we sailed back home again. I was a little sad to say goodbye to Lach, but mostly I was just lonely. Besides Uncle Will on the other end of Hypoluxo Island, our nearest neighbors were a boat ride away. There were no other kids anywhere near our house, and I missed Tiger Bowlegs every day.

Our life on Lake Worth was simple in lots of ways. Papa didn't have any glass when he built our house, so our windows were just open holes in the walls with curtains and shutters. This did nothing to keep the mosquitoes out. At night, we couldn't light candles or lanterns because the light attracted mosquitoes. You could almost hear them buzzing in your sleep. The worst mosquitoes were called no-see-ums. No-see-ums were very tiny mosquitoes with a very big bite. Mama said she was nearly driven crazy by no-see-ums because they were impossible to see. So we burned smudge pots that filled the house with foul-smelling smoke to keep the mosquitoes away. We spent many a night sitting in our dark house, inhaling smudge pot fumes while remembering our family and friends back in Chicago.

Our condition distressed our relatives. Papa's family in New England could not understand why we chose to live in such primitive conditions. Mama's family was even more worried. Her mother was a school teacher and was afraid that I was being raised with no education. As a result, they sent books whenever they could. The problem was that there was no regular mail service. The nearest post office was 120 miles north at Sand Point. Sometimes we didn't receive mail for months at a time, only when Papa or someone else on the lake sailed to Sand Point or when someone sailed down with a bundle of mail.

Grandma didn't have to worry. Mama almost never missed a chance to give me a lesson. She taught me grammar, reading, mathematics, and science, and I read more books than most children my age would have ever read back in Chicago. I especially liked the Greek myths, and I also read a new book called *Roughing It*, by Mark Twain. It was about Mr. Twain's travels through the West. I wondered what Mr. Twain would think of being stuck in a hurricane all night.

When I wasn't working with Mama, Papa taught me about the stars and how clouds make rain and how the moon pulls on the ocean to create tides. When we started planting, I worked with Papa in the vegetable patch, and he taught me about crossing different kinds of plants with each other to make new, stronger kinds. I was also a crack shot with my rifle, could tie any type of knot, rig any sail, and pilot any boat, and I had learned to speak some Miccosukee, the language of the Seminoles. Life on Lake Worth was not bad at all. It was just different.

Chapter Ten

Orange Grove House of Refuge

In late 1875, the United States Life Saving Service announced that it was building five buildings along the lower east coast of Florida for the purpose of housing shipwrecked persons. The buildings would be called Houses of Refuge. The northernmost House of Refuge was built first, along Bethel Creek in what is now Vero Beach. The second House of Refuge was called Gilbert's Bar and was about fifteen miles north of the Jupiter Lighthouse.

In the winter of 1876, the federal government began construction of House of Refuge Number 3, which became known as the Orange Grove House of Refuge because it was located near a grove of sour wild oranges that some believe the Spanish had planted several hundred years ago. It was built along a wide stretch of beach about eight miles south of our house on Hypoluxo Island. Many years later the area around the Orange Grove House would become known as Delray Beach.

The Orange Grove House was completed in late April 1876 and needed a fulltime keeper. Papa agreed to become the first keeper, and we moved in the first week of May. The move was a little disruptive because we were now used to our home on Hypoluxo Island, where Uncle Will lived on the other end of the island, and we had neighbors a few miles up the lake. At the Orange Grove House, we would have no neighbors at all. Moreover, Mama was expecting a baby in three months. An isolated house on the beach was no place to give birth to a baby.

Before we moved south to the House of Refuge, Papa sent for a Negro lady named Aunt Betsy. Aunt Betsy was not really my aunt, but we called her that. She had been a slave and had escaped to Florida from her master's plantation in Georgia during the Civil War. Papa and Mama had befriended her during the brief time that we lived near Fort Pierce. Papa wanted Aunt Betsy to come down from her home on the Indian River near Fort Pierce and take care of our house on Hypoluxo Island while we were at the Orange Grove House. Just about the time we were ready to move, Aunt Betsy arrived. We left the house on Hypoluxo Island in her capable hands and moved south to Papa's new job on the beach.

Life at the Orange Grove House was exciting. I spent my days on the beach, fishing, collecting turtle eggs, and hunting in the Spanish River Lagoon on the other side of the beach ridge to the west. Nights were spent

enjoying the gentle breezes rolling off the ocean. During May, June, and July, the giant loggerhead, green, and leatherback turtles came ashore at night to lay their eggs. Each morning, I would find fresh mounds of sand containing sometimes hundreds of large turtle eggs. Turtle eggs became a staple in our diet, as did turtle meat. Mama made an excellent turtle stew.

It turned out we weren't the only ones who liked turtle eggs. Almost every evening during turtle nesting season, black bears would come over the beach dunes from the woods, looking for nests of fresh turtle eggs. When they found a nest, the bears would patiently dig up and crack open the eggs, drinking the contents from the eggshell like a human drinking out of a coconut. Every once in a while, Papa would shoot a bear if it got too close to the House of Refuge. When he did, we ate bear steaks and salted the rest of the meat to save it.

One day, I was down on the beach when I heard a familiar voice calling, "Charlie! Charlie!" I turned around and could scarcely believe my eyes. Tiger Bowlegs was coming over the beach dune after he and his father had stopped at the Orange Grove House. I knew the Seminoles traveled the Spanish River, and I had hoped to one day see Tiger Bowlegs again, but I was still surprised.

"You taller," he said, looking up at me and grinning.

"You're not," I answered, laughing a little.

"Maybe no, but I still wrestle you."

Tiger's father agreed they could stay for a few days. Papa said they could stay in the House of Refuge. We had plenty of room, as the attic was designed to sleep up to twenty shipwreck victims at a time. But Tiger's father refused to sleep in a house. Instead, Tiger and his father camped on the beach. That first night, Mama let me sleep on the beach with Tiger and his father, and we sat by the small fire until the moon was high in the sky.

The next morning, Tiger and I set out just after dawn in his dugout canoe. I had Ol' Lauderdale with me, and we were hoping to track some buck. Tiger said he and his father had seen deer droppings up the river, and he thought there was a big buck in the area. We found a good place to hide in the pines and waited silently for a few hours until, finally, a huge buck appeared in a break in the trees. It was by far the biggest deer I'd ever seen, and I raised my rifle to shoot.

But Tiger held up his hand and motioned for me to stop. He nodded at me, and his dark eyes glittered with excitement. Wait, he was saying.

So I waited. It seemed like it took forever, but the big buck slowly began to pick his way toward us, through the woods. As he got nearer, my heart pounded with excitement. He had a ten-point rack, and he must have weighed at least 250 pounds. I'd never even heard of a buck that big in South Florida. Finally, Tiger nodded to me, and in one swift motion, I raised the rifle, sighted along the barrel, and dropped the deer with one shot to the neck.

"Nice shoot," Tiger said approvingly. "You make good Indian."

We dragged our prize buck back to the canoe. He was so heavy that we could drag him only a few feet at a time. When we put him into the canoe, the canoe almost sank.

Pretty soon, we were back at the House of Refuge, and I was excited to show Papa our deer. Papa wasn't outside, as I expected, so I ran up to the house. Papa met me at the door, and I knew right away that something was going on. Papa looked as if he'd seen a ghost, and he wasn't paying attention when I told him I shot a huge deer.

"What's going on, Papa?" I asked.

Then he smiled. "Charlie," he said, "you've got a baby sister!" It turns out Mama had gone into labor while I was gone and given birth to Lillie Elder. It was August 1876, and Lillie was the first white girl ever born between Jupiter and Miami. I decided that my deer was a good sign, and I told Papa that we could put the rack of antlers in Lillie's room so that the spirit of the giant buck would watch over her. He thought that was a fine idea, and later that day,

he and Tiger's father helped us dress out the deer. As was the custom, we split the meat, and Tiger's father ended up taking as much as he could carry.

The next morning, Mama took very ill. She lay in bed with a high fever, shaking and sweating in bed. Papa tried everything he knew, but it wasn't working, so he called me into the room. Mama was white like a sheet, and when I got near her, I could feel the heat pouring from her skin. "Go get Aunt Betsy!" Papa ordered.

I ran up the beach as fast as I could go. I ran the entire eight miles and swam across the lake to Hypoluxo Island. Getting Aunt Betsy back was a lot slower, as she was overweight and middle-aged and not used to walking in the soft sand along the beach. I ended up carrying her big cloth sack of herbs and potions.

When we got back to the House of Refuge, Aunt Betsy took one look at Mama and shook her head. "Don' know if I can help her, but I'll try," she said. Aunt Betsy knew slave medicine, or African medicine. She fished in her bag and withdrew a few small sacks of herbs. She crushed them first, then boiled them together. It smelled awful, and I think Papa was afraid to ask what was in that potion. When she was done, she strained the potion through a white sheet, muttered a few words over it, then told Papa it was "good African medicine" and to give the drink to Mama right away.

Mama could barely drink it, and it looked as if she might spit it back out. But eventually she swallowed it all. Then she went right to sleep. She slept for almost twenty-four hours straight. Father was fit to be tied waiting for her to wake up. He did not eat or sleep a wink. I knew what he was thinking. He was angry at himself again. Why had he brought his beautiful wife to this wilderness, where there were no doctors and no hospitals? How would he live without her if she died? Who would raise Lillie? How would he explain her death to Uncle Will and Mama's parents? He nearly paced a hole into the floor of the House of Refuge.

Then the following day, Mama woke up and, although tired, was nearly her old self again. She slowly regained her strength over the next couple of weeks, and Aunt Betsy stayed by her side until she was almost fully recovered. After two weeks, I walked Aunt Betsy back up the beach, across the lake, and to the house on Hypoluxo Island. By anyone's estimation, Aunt Betsy had saved Mama's life.

Chapter Eleven

The "Big Rain"

After Mama was better, Papa announced he had to sail up to Sand Point to restock our supplies. It was late summer, and we were running low. While he was gone, the rest of us—me, Mama, and Lillie—were going to move back to the house on Hypoluxo Island and live with Aunt Betsy. He figured he would be gone a couple of weeks.

Not much had changed on Hypoluxo Island, but Uncle Will said that more and more people were coming into the area to homestead. A week later, I saw what he meant when I spotted a boat filled with men, women, and children heading south down the lake, toward the island. The boat contained the Dimick and Geer families. They were from Illinois and had just arrived to take up homesteads further north.

They had sailed down from St. Augustine with all their furniture and possessions loaded on a large sailboat, which was anchored offshore. They planned to raft all their furniture and possessions ashore, then store everything someplace dry while they built houses for themselves. When Uncle Will heard this, he said they better get their stuff off their sailboat real quick because the weather in September can be dangerous.

For the next three days, Uncle Will helped the Dimicks and the Geers unload their possessions. They stashed some of their things in the hammocks on the west side of the beach dune, and they brought some to our house. We didn't know either family before this, but we were happy to help out. They were pioneer settlers like us, and Papa always said it was important to help all the pioneers, especially ones who were about to become neighbors.

I'd never met families as tight as the Dimicks and the Geers. I couldn't keep it all straight, because it seemed that every Dimick was a cousin or in-law to every Geer. Mama explained it a few times. She said that two Dimick brothers had married sisters from the Geer family, and one Geer man had married a Dimick woman. So all six of the adults were either siblings or in-laws, and all of their children were cousins. There were thirteen of them in all.

Mama somehow found space in the house for all the women and children. The men camped outside in the yard.

A few days after they arrived, I was at the north end of the island helping Uncle Will rig his sailing skiff when two Seminoles pulled along the shoreline in a canoe. As usual, we did not see or hear them coming. I first thought they were here to trade with us, but I saw their canoe was empty. Uncle Will greeted them. "What can I do for you?" he asked.

One of the Seminoles shaded his eyes against the sun. "Here to warn you," he said. "Flowers on sawgrass closing up. This means big rain coming." Uncle Will looked alarmed even though the sun was shining and the only wind was a gentle breeze from the northwest. Big rain was their term for a hurricane, and we knew better than to doubt the Seminoles. Personally, I would have been happy to never see another hurricane after my first one.

"Thank you," Uncle Will said, and the

Seminoles got back into their canoe and paddled west, back toward the Everglades.

Unfortunately, there wasn't much we could do to protect ourselves if a hurricane really was coming. The house was already jammed full of people and their things, so we cleaned up the property the best we could, tied down the boats, folded and packed the sails, and hoped the Seminoles were wrong. But they weren't. By the early afternoon, the wind had changed directions, and the skies turned black. Uncle Will and I ran for the house.

The Dimicks and the Geers had no idea what a hurricane was, but they looked plenty scared. Uncle Will and I were tying their furniture down on the porch when I spotted

Papa sailing down the lake toward us. Papa looked intense, and he had his full sails out and was running before the wind as fast as he could. He tied up the boat, jumped ashore, and said that he had just come from the Jupiter Lighthouse on his way back from Sand Point. While at the lighthouse, he saw Tiger's father, who told him a hurricane was coming. Papa knew to listen to the Seminoles as they had been accurately predicting the weather for generations.

After we tied everything down, there was nothing to do but wait and hope. So we sat in the darkness, with a few candles flickering, and prayed while Aunt Betsy sang quietly. But the storm came upon us quickly, just like the first time. By four o'clock, the winds were howling,

and the rain was being driven horizontally across the yard. In the midst of all this, several other families from further up the lake arrived at our house and begged us to give them shelter. They knew that Papa had built the sturdiest home anywhere in South Florida. Of course, Mama and Papa welcomed them into our already full house. By nightfall, twenty-one people were in the house, including the children. This was probably the largest single gathering of settlers in South Florida up until that time.

Pretty soon, I could hear the wind whistling through the branches outside. I knew this was the sign of a big hurricane. Only the big ones have strong enough wind to cause a high-pitched whistle. It was a strange and awful sound, and it struck fear into us. Every time thunder boomed outside, I jumped. Underneath the whistling, I heard the steady roar of waves pounding the beach and rain and lake water battering the house. The house itself shivered, and it felt as if the whole structure might lift off its foundation and fly into the lake.

Papa and I tried to keep the newcomers calm, but it was hard to act brave when I was nervous, too. At one point, Papa tried to tell them that he was "not worried about the house blowing down as long as the trees were still standing." But then I peeked outside the shutters and saw that every tree in our yard had been snapped in half. The trunks of some of the great mastic and banyan trees were at least eight feet thick in the middle and at least two

hundred years old. I immediately closed the window and didn't tell anyone what I had seen.

At about two o'clock in the morning, the winds shifted, and we knew that we were now on the backside of the hurricane. The eye of the storm must have passed to the south of us. We spent the rest of the night listening to the strong winds and trying to sleep.

By daybreak, the rains had ended and the winds were calm. It had been a long, tiring night, and some of the smaller children were still sleeping. A few of the adults and I wandered outside, and we could scarcely believe our eyes. Every single tree had been felled and every plant stripped clean of leaves. There was hardly anything green left. Our vegetable patch was

completely destroyed. Worse yet, everything the Dimicks and the Geers had left on our porch was spread far and wide down the island. One of their dressers was even floating in the lake.

After helping the Dimicks and the Geers collect their possessions, or at least what was left of them, I crossed the lake and went over the beach dune to see what the hurricane might have deposited on the beach or whether any ships had been wrecked and people were in need of help.

Fortunately, there were no shipwreck victims in need of aid. Unfortunately, there was not a single item of cargo on the beach to be salvaged. There were fish of every color, size, and variety, which we collected and took home to eat. Later that day, Will Lanehart, a pioneer settler who lived north of us, came down the beach with a flamingo he had killed. Flamingos were not native to this area, and all we could figure is that the hurricane carried it over from the Bahama Islands.

Chapter Twelve

Our Lady of Santa Marta

I couldn't believe the destruction the hurricane had caused along the beach. Before the storm, the beach was probably a thousand feet wide from the water line to the top of the beach dune. After the storm, it was only about two hundred feet wide. In addition, sand to a depth of at least ten feet had been washed away, and I could see huge rocks and ancient reefs that used to be covered by sand.

It wasn't just I who was confused. Many deer, bear, and wild hogs were wandering aimlessly around the beach dune. I guess they were confused and lost. Most animals use smells to mark the boundaries of their territories. As best I could figure, the storm stripped the leaves, branches, and bark off nearly every tree and bush and probably removed whatever scent the animals used to define boundaries and navigate by.

I walked for miles up the beach toward Jupiter, hoping to find something that had washed up. About halfway between Hypoluxo Island and the Jupiter Inlet, I saw an odd-shaped structure sticking out of the ground in the middle of the beach. Even from a distance, I knew it couldn't be a rock. As I got closer, I realized it was a piece of a shipwreck. Finally, I might find something of value as a result of this disastrous storm.

But this ship looked very odd. It didn't look like any ship I had ever seen before. And it was mostly buried in the middle of the beach. How was this possible? How did the storm push a ship this far ashore and then bury it with sand at the same time the storm was eroding ten feet of sand from the beach?

I got on my hands and knees and began digging around the edges. I dug for almost an hour, trying to find the edges of the broken hull. I dug until I uncovered some writing on the hull. I could make out the words but did not know what they meant. It said *Nuestra Señora de Santa Marta*. I had no idea what the words meant, but I kept digging.

In another few minutes, my fingers hit something hard. I soon uncovered the top of a box lying next to the hull. I dug faster, and before long, I could see the whole box. Actually, it was a chest. I tried to lift it, but it was too heavy. The chest was about three feet long by two feet wide, with a large metal latch inscribed with a cross. Since I couldn't move it, I lifted the latch and pushed the lid up.

I couldn't believe what I was looking at! The entire chest was filled with hundreds of sparkling gold coins. They were unlike any coins I had ever seen. Each coin had a cross on one side surrounded by strange markings and words that I could not understand. What I could understand, though, were the words *Philip V* and the dates, which ranged from 1711 to 1715.

The chest was too heavy to lift or to carry, so I reburied it. I took one coin with me and ran as fast as I could back down the beach toward Hypoluxo Island. When I arrived at the house, I learned that Papa had already set sail back to the House of Refuge, and the Dimicks and the Geers were up the lake at their homesteads, beginning to clear the land to

build their houses. This was just as well because it would not have been wise to tell everyone about the treasure I had found.

I told Mama the story of my find. I am not sure that she believed me until I showed her the coin that I brought back with me. When she saw it, her eyes grew large and she took it slowly from my hand. "Mercy!" she said and caught her breath.

"What is it?"

She flipped it over and bounced it in her hand. "Charlie, you better go get your Uncle Will right now. And don't tell anyone else about this!"

I found Uncle Will repairing hurricane damage to his house. When I told him I found a buried trunk full of golden coins, he dropped his hammer onto the ground and hurried back with me. Along the way, he asked me every kind of question he could think of about the buried ship and the coins. When he saw the coin, he looked even more shocked than Mama. He bit it and left tooth marks in the metal. "Charlie," he said, "this is gold. How many of these are there?"

"I don't know," I answered. "A few hundred, I guess."

"A few hundred!" Uncle Will looked like he was about to fall over. He wanted to leave right then to go back to the shipwreck, but Mama announced it was too dark for us to walk up the beach alone, especially with confused animals roaming around. Uncle Will said he knew that

Philip V was the king of Spain in the early 1700s, but he had no idea what a Spanish ship with a chest full of gold coins was doing buried on the beach in Florida.

I hardly slept that night. As soon as the sun broke over the horizon, I was dressed and out the door, running up the muddy trail that connected our house to Uncle Will's. Together, we rowed Uncle Will's small boat, *Bessie B*, across the lake, hiked through the jungle on the beach ridge, and began our long walk north. Uncle Will brought ropes and a knife so that we could cut some branches, bind them together into a sled, and drag the chest home. It took us several hours to reach the wreck site. Less of the ship was visible than the day before. The ocean was already beginning a steady reburial of the ship, with each crashing wave at high tide depositing more sand on the beach.

It took a little extra digging to find the chest, but I didn't care about the extra work as long as we found it. While I dug, Uncle Will searched the jungle on the other side of the beach dune for sturdy tree limbs to construct the sled. After a couple hours' work, the chest was out of the ground, and the sled was built.

We wanted to dig around the wreck site to look for other possible treasure, but it was getting late, and we were worried that dragging the heavy sled would put us home after dark. We decided to head home and return the next day to look for more loot.

We arrived home just after nightfall. Mama had sent a message down to the Orange Grove House with one of the Geer boys shortly after Uncle Will and I had left that morning. The message said nothing of the treasure. It only said "URGENT, return home at once." So by the time Uncle Will and I dragged the chest out of the *Bessie B* and up the porch steps, Papa was standing on the porch waiting for us.

We brought the chest into the house, opened it, and began sorting through the coins by candlelight. We counted 456 solid gold coins. Papa said that any one of them would make a poor man rich. Then Papa remembered a story he'd heard from Captain Armour, who had heard it from treasure hunters passing by the lighthouse.

In late July 1715, a flotilla of eleven Spanish ships, each loaded with gold, silver, and emeralds from South America, set sail from Havana, Cuba. But a few days into the voyage back to Spain, the fleet was thrown off course by a massive hurricane and smashed into the shallow reefs off Florida's east coast. More than one thousand Spanish sailors died, and all eleven ships were destroyed. The Spanish sent rescue and salvage ships from Havana and the Spanish fort, Castillo de San Marcos, in St. Augustine, to rescue the survivors and salvage the treasure. However, the Spanish were able to locate only ten of the eleven ships. The ship they never found was named *Nuestra Señora de Santa Marta*, which means Our Lady of Santa Marta.

"That's the name of the ship I found!" I exclaimed.

Papa speculated that the Spanish never found the *Santa Marta* because it was much farther south than the ten other Spanish ships, which had wrecked along the beaches from the St. Lucie Inlet to the Sebastian Inlet. The Spanish probably had not thought to look so far south. Then the ship was buried under ten feet of sand and disappeared.

We inspected each of the 456 coins very closely. Over time, Papa and Mama ordered books about Spanish coins. They also sent sketches of the coins to one of Papa's brothers who was a professor at Harvard, near Boston, Massachusetts. After many months of ordering and reading books and corresponding with professors at Harvard, we learned that the coins were all made in Mexico and Nueva Granada (modern-day Colombia) between the years 1711 and 1715. The words on the coins translated to "Philip V by the grace of God King of Spain and the Indies." Also, each coin was marked with "8 S," which meant eight *escudos*. These were the largest gold coins made by the Spanish and were referred to as "doubloons" by the English colonists because the coin was double the value of the four escudo coin. Forever afterward, our family simply referred to them as doubloons.

After a long night of counting and inspecting the coins, we went to bed. We planned to return to the wreck site the next day with Papa and shovels to see what else we could find.

But we were awakened the next morning by a howling wind that slammed the shutters against the side of the house. The rain and strong winds lasted all day and into the next night. We couldn't go on our treasure search. The next day came and went, and it was still pouring rain. The third day came and went with no relief in sight. By the fourth day, the strong storm had passed and the sun was shining. Papa, Uncle Will, and I packed our digging tools and headed north, up the beach.

However, the beach was totally different. The three straight days of wind and waves from the northeast had returned all the sand to the beach. We could not find the wreck of the *Santa Marta*. We searched in vain for hours, only to run out of daylight.

We returned day after day, but to no avail. The autumn storms continued to pile more and more sand on the beach, burying our treasure ship deeper and deeper. As the foliage returned to the beach dune, it became more and more difficult for us to be certain we were even digging at the right part of the beach.

After several weeks of searching in vain, Papa had to return to his job at the House of Refuge. Mama, Lillie, and I went with Papa back to the Orange Grove House. Uncle Will returned to farming and tending to his gardens. The chest of 456 doubloons was buried in our backyard at the foot of a giant banyan tree and dug up only periodically over the next three generations, whenever someone needed to pay for something very important, such as more land or a new sailing boat.

As for the *Santa Marta*, she is still there, buried since August 1715 in the sands of the beach between Hypoluxo Island and the Jupiter Inlet. Her remaining treasure, estimated by the Spanish crown to have been worth millions, has never been found. Her final resting place was known only by my family, and we never told anyone.

About Charlie Pierce

Charles William Pierce was born in Waukegan, Illinois in 1864 and moved with his parents to Jupiter, Florida in 1872 at the age of eight years, when his father was given the job as assistant keeper of the Jupiter Lighthouse. At the time, the geographical area that today is Palm Beach County was still part of Dade County (Palm Beach County was not created until 1909) and was largely inhabited only by Native Americans and a few escaped former slaves.

Left to right: Hannibal D. Pierce; his wife, Margretta M. Pierce; Andrew W. Garnett; James "Ed" Hamilton; Lillie E. Pierce; and Charles W. Pierce at the Pierce family home on Hypoluxo Island.

The Pierce family homesteaded Hypoluxo Island in 1873. In 1876, Charlie's father served as the first keeper of the Orange Grove House of Refuge, (in modern-day Delray Beach), where the Pierce family housed shipwrecked sailors along the beach. It was here that Charlie's sister, Lillie, was born in August 1876. She was the first non–Native American child born between Jupiter and Miami, an area that contains approximately 7 million people today.

Pierce grew up in the jungle wilderness that was South Florida prior to the arrival of Henry Flagler's Florida East Coast Railroad some two decades later. The Pierces were one of the three families that salvaged the 1878 wreck of the *Providencia*, a Spanish ship carrying 20,000 coconuts. The Pierces helped plant the coconuts that would later give Palm Beach, West Palm Beach, and Palm Beach County their names.

During his long, illustrious life as a pioneer settler of South Florida, Pierce served in many capacities, most notably as one of the legendary Barefoot Mailmen who carried the mail from Palm Beach to Miami and back each week. In all, the Barefoot Mailmen covered 136 round-trip miles in six days, rested on Sunday, and then began again on Monday, a total of approximately 7,000 miles per year. They were paid $600 per year.

Pierce served for over forty years as the postmaster of Boynton Beach, moving to Boynton Beach in 1895, over twenty years before the city was first incorporated. His son, Charles, was the first child born in Boynton Beach. Pierce served on the boards of various community organizations. He was president of the first bank organized in Boynton Beach and master of the first Masonic Lodge.

The mailman in this mural titled *The Barefoot Mailman*, by Stevan Dohanos, is said to resemble Charlie Pierce. *Photo courtesy of Historical Society of Palm Beach County*

His childhood adventures were accurately recorded, and his writings remain one of the best firsthand accounts of early exploration in Southeast Florida. Pierce was farsighted enough to maintain a daily journal from early childhood until late in his life. These journal entries provide the foundation for his book, *Pioneer Life in Southeast Florida*, which is the most comprehensive account of the pioneer settlement of south Florida and one of the primary references for most subsequent books on the region's history.

Pierce died in 1939, at age seventy-five, while still serving as the Postmaster of Boynton Beach. Pierce Hammock Elementary School, in Palm Beach County, is named in his honor. In 2009, the State of Florida posthumously named Charles Pierce a Great Floridian, one of fewer than forty-five people in Florida's history granted the title. Florida Governor Charlie Crist performed the induction.

Charles Pierce at his desk, circa 1930. *Photo courtesy of Historical Society of Palm Beach County*

Harvey E. Oyer III

Harvey E. Oyer III is a fifth-generation Floridian and is descended from one of the earliest pioneer families in South Florida. He is the great-great-grandson of Captain Hannibal Dillingham Pierce and his wife, Margretta Moore Pierce, who in 1872 became one of the first non–Native American families to settle in Southeast Florida. Oyer is the great grandnephew of Charlie Pierce, the subject of this book.

Oyer is an attorney in West Palm Beach, Florida; a Cambridge University–educated archaeologist; and an avid historian. He served for many years as the chairman of the Historical Society of Palm Beach County and has written or contributed to numerous books and articles about Florida history. Many of the stories contained in this book have been passed down through five generations of his family.

For more information about the author, Harvey E. Oyer III, or Charlie Pierce and his adventures, go to **www.TheAdventuresofCharliePierce.com**
Become a friend of Charlie Pierce on **Facebook**
Facebook.com/CharliePierceBooks

Visit The Adventures of Charlie Pierce website at
www.TheAdventuresofCharliePierce.com

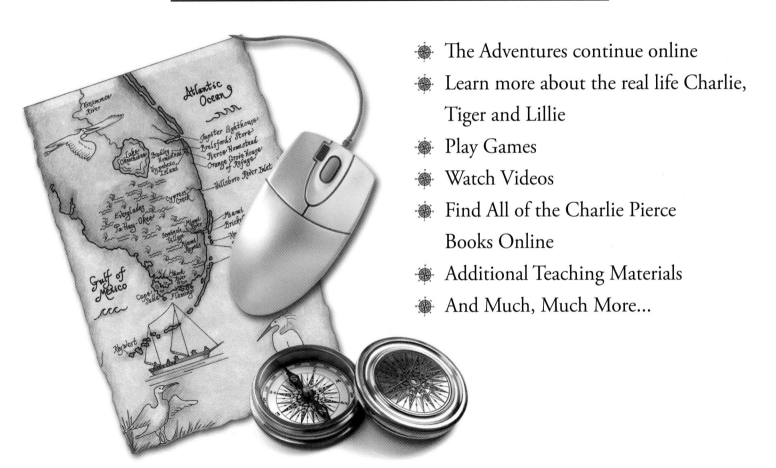

- The Adventures continue online
- Learn more about the real life Charlie, Tiger and Lillie
- Play Games
- Watch Videos
- Find All of the Charlie Pierce Books Online
- Additional Teaching Materials
- And Much, Much More...

The Adventures of Charlie Pierce Collection

The Adventures of Charlie Pierce: The American Jungle

In 1872, eight-year-old Charlie Pierce arrived with his Mama and Papa in the frontier jungles of South Florida. In this account, based on actual diaries, Charlie explores old battlefields, faces down hurricanes, and makes an incredible discovery in the sand.

The Adventures of Charlie Pierce: The Last Egret

In the late nineteenth century, hunters killed millions of birds in the Florida Everglades to supply the booming trade in bird feathers for ladies' fashion. As teenagers, Charlie Pierce and his friends traveled deep into the unexplored Florida Everglades to hunt plume birds for their feathers. They never imagined what they would learn about themselves and how they would contribute to American history.

The Adventures of Charlie Pierce: The Last Calusa

When famous scientist Dr. George Livingston shows up in the steamy jungles of Florida, he offers to pay Charlie Pierce to take him deep into the Everglades in search of the rare ghost orchid. But it doesn't take long before the expedition discovers that the swamp is hiding much more than a rare flower as the oldest legends suddenly spring to life.

The Adventures of Charlie Pierce: The Barefoot Mailman

Charlie Pierce isn't looking for an adventure when he agrees to help out his friend and neighbor Ed Hamilton. Hamilton's job is to walk the U.S. Mail from Palm Beach to Miami and back every week. When Hamilton goes missing, it's up to Charlie and his sister, Lillie, to find out what happened to the missing Barefoot Mailman.

The Adventures of Charlie Pierce: Charlie and the Tycoon

When industrialist Henry Flagler arrives in Florida in the late 19th century, the state is a wild jungle with few people. But that changes quickly as Flagler builds hotels and railroads down the Atlantic coast—with the help of teenaged Charlie Pierce. Along the way, Charlie and his family realize that building the future means saying goodbye to the Florida they know and love.

Awards for The Adventures of Charlie Pierce

Florida Publishers Association
Gold Medal - Children's Fiction (*The American Jungle,* 2010)
Gold Medal - Florida Children's Book (*The American Jungle,* 2010)
Gold Medal - Children's Fiction (*The Last Egret,* 2011)
Silver Medal - Florida Children's Book (*The Last Egret,* 2011)
Gold Medal - Florida Children's Book (*The Last Calusa,* 2013)
Silver Medal - Children's Fiction (*The Last Calusa,* 2013)
Gold Medal - Fiction/Non-Fiction: Juvenile (*The Barefoot Mailman,* 2015)

James J. Horgan Award (Florida Historical Society)
(*The Last Egret,* 2011)
(*The Last Calusa,* 2013)

Florida Book Award
Bronze Medal - Children's Literature (*The Last Egret,* 2010)

Mom's Choice Awards
Silver Medal (*The Last Egret,* 2010)

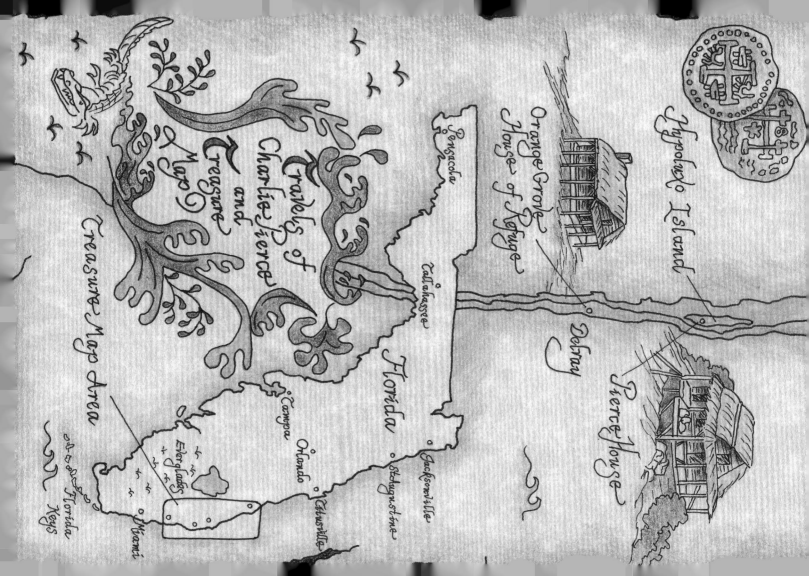

Travels of Charlie Pierce and Treasure Map

Treasure Map Area

Florida Keys

Florida

Pensacola

Tallahassee

Tampa

Orlando

Everglades

Miami

Titusville

Jacksonville

St. Augustine

Delray

Orange Grove House of Refuge

Pierce House

Hypoluxo Island